randomhousekids.com
ISBN 978-1-101-93464-7
Printed in the United States of America
10 9 8 7 6 5 4 3 2 1

Based on the teleplay "Blast to the Past"
by Brandon Auman

Illustrated by Paul Linsley

 A GOLDEN BOOK · NEW YORK

One dark night, the Teenage Mutant Ninja Turtles were in the Party Wagon, tracking the villain Tiger Claw and his henchmen Bebop and Rocksteady. The path led to the Museum of Natural History.

Leo looked at his brothers. "Four peanut butter and pepperoni pizzas says they're out to steal something."

The Turtles followed the bad guys into the museum.

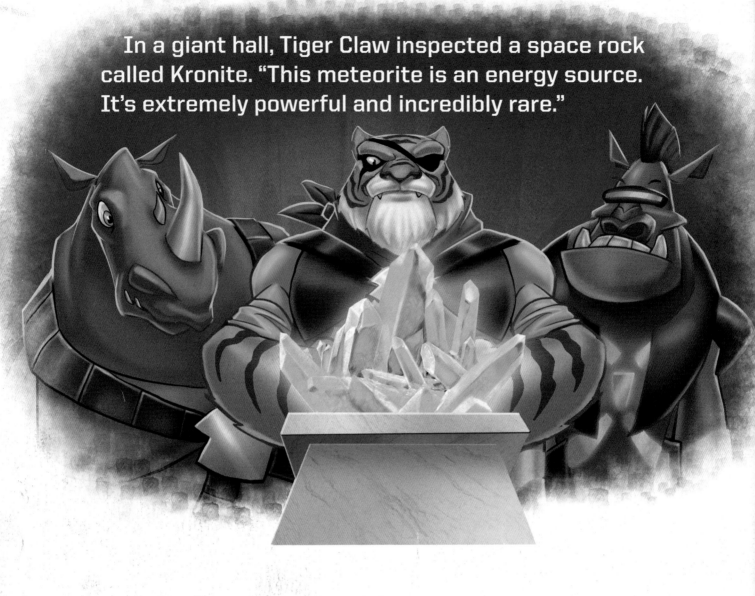

In a giant hall, Tiger Claw inspected a space rock called Kronite. "This meteorite is an energy source. It's extremely powerful and incredibly rare."

Crouching in the dark, Mikey was amazed by the dinosaur bones on display.

"Don't touch anything," Raph whispered.

But it was too late. Mikey nudged a toe bone and an entire T. rex skeleton crashed to the ground.

Tiger Claw and his henchmen charged at the Turtles.

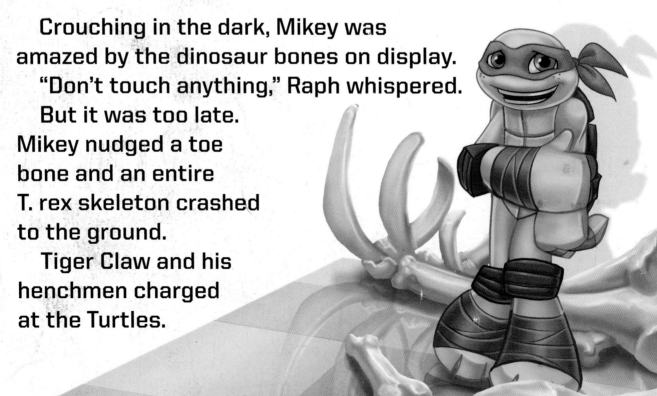

Leo sliced another skeleton with his twin swords.
The bones collapsed on top of the bad guys.
Raph grabbed the meteorite. "Let's haul shell!"
Mikey threw down a smoke bomb, and the
Turtles escaped.

Back in the lair, Donnie examined the Kronite. "The power this thing emits is off the chizzart!" Suddenly, he had an idea. Maybe the meteorite could power his new project—the Shellformer. It was a vehicle that could fly, roll on treads, and transform into a giant turtle-bot!

The Turtles climbed into the Shellformer for a test ride. Donnie powered up the ship with meteorite crystals and set it to rocket-jet mode.

Rocksteady and Bebop were watching from the shadows. They wanted to get the meteorite back, so they leaped onto the ship as it blasted off!

The crystals were way stronger than Donnie expected. When the Shellformer came to a stop, the Turtles discovered they had gone back in time to the age of the dinosaurs!

Bebop and Rocksteady jumped off the ship and hid in the woods.

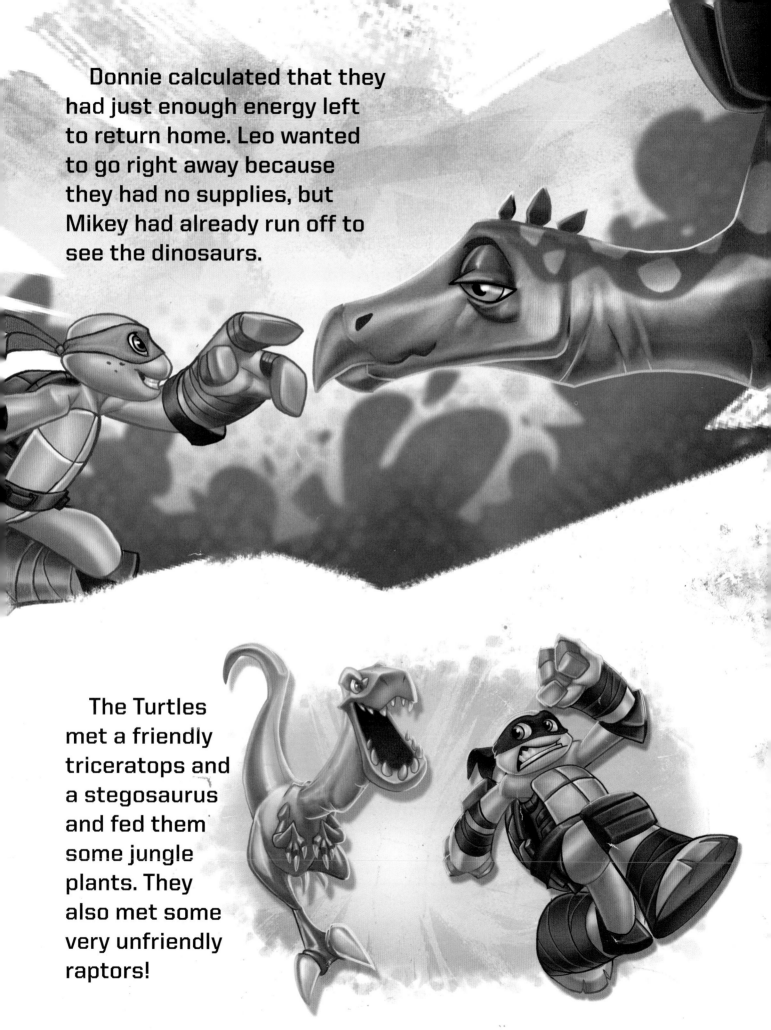

Donnie calculated that they had just enough energy left to return home. Leo wanted to go right away because they had no supplies, but Mikey had already run off to see the dinosaurs.

The Turtles met a friendly triceratops and a stegosaurus and fed them some jungle plants. They also met some very unfriendly raptors!

Luckily, the raptors ran away—when a hungry
T. rex crashed through the bushes! *"ROAAAR!"*
   "We can't stop a T. rex with sticks and blades!"
Donnie shouted.
   "RUN!" Leo yelled.

Suddenly, a giant pteranodon swooped out of the sky and took Raph for a ride. They accidentally crashed into a tree and the dinosaur hurt her wing.

"Easy now," Raph said. "I'll fix you up with my med kit."

When Raph finished wrapping the bandage, the creature squawked a cry of thanks and flew away.

The Turtles returned to the Shellformer. But before they could take off, two T. rexes attacked. Donnie transformed their ship into the TURTLEBOT 5000 and fought back.

A giant zap of electricity sent the dinosaurs running, but it also drained the ship's power. The Turtles were stuck in the dinosaur era.

As the Turtles worked on a plan to get home, they made a shocking discovery—evil aliens called Triceratons had a base in the prehistoric jungle. They were mining crystals from the original Kronite meteorite!

Donnie could see that there were just enough crystals to send the Shellformer home. But how would the Turtles get them? "Intruders!" a Triceraton guard yelled as he spotted the Turtles.

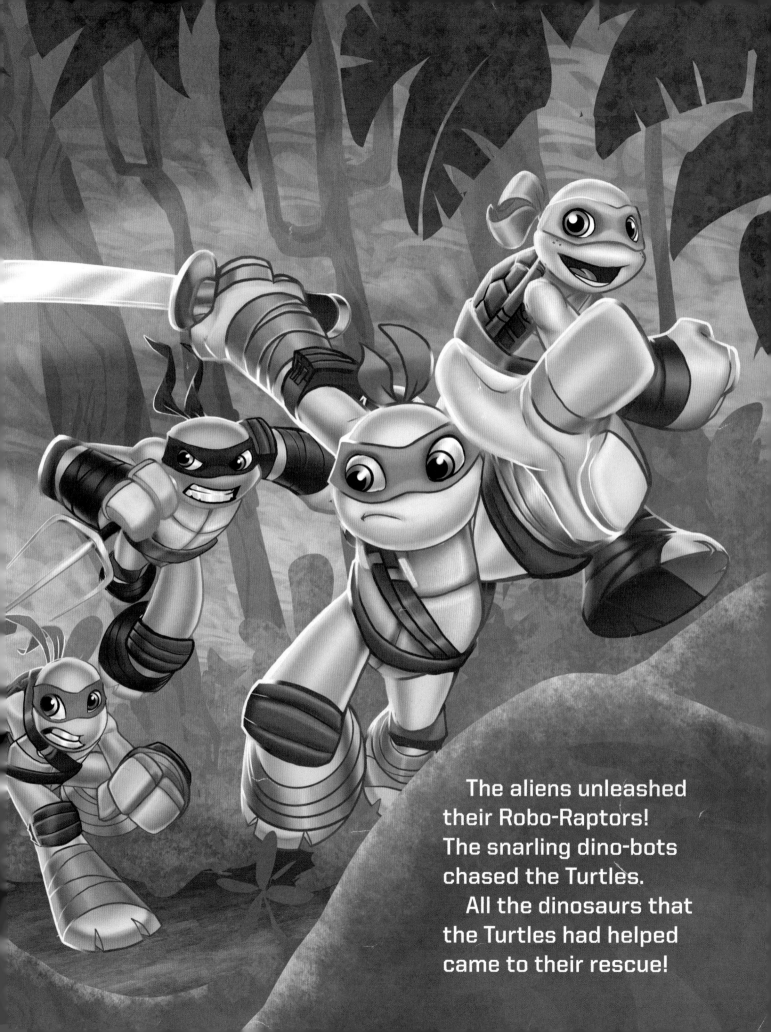

The aliens unleashed
their Robo-Raptors!
The snarling dino-bots
chased the Turtles.
All the dinosaurs that
the Turtles had helped
came to their rescue!

Just when the Turtles had escaped the Robo-Raptors, a T. rex cornered them in a dark cave.

Mikey handed Donnie an old piece of pizza he had been carrying. "No animal in any time period can resist pepperoni, maple syrup, and sprinkles!"

Donnie held out the slice, and the dinosaur slurped it up. The Turtles had a new—and very large—friend.

Meanwhile, Bebop and Rocksteady had been captured by the Triceratons and brought to the alien leader, General Zera. She wanted to use the meteorite crystals to move through time, waging war and taking over the universe.

Bebop and Rocksteady knew they had to escape, even if it meant teaming up with the Turtles.

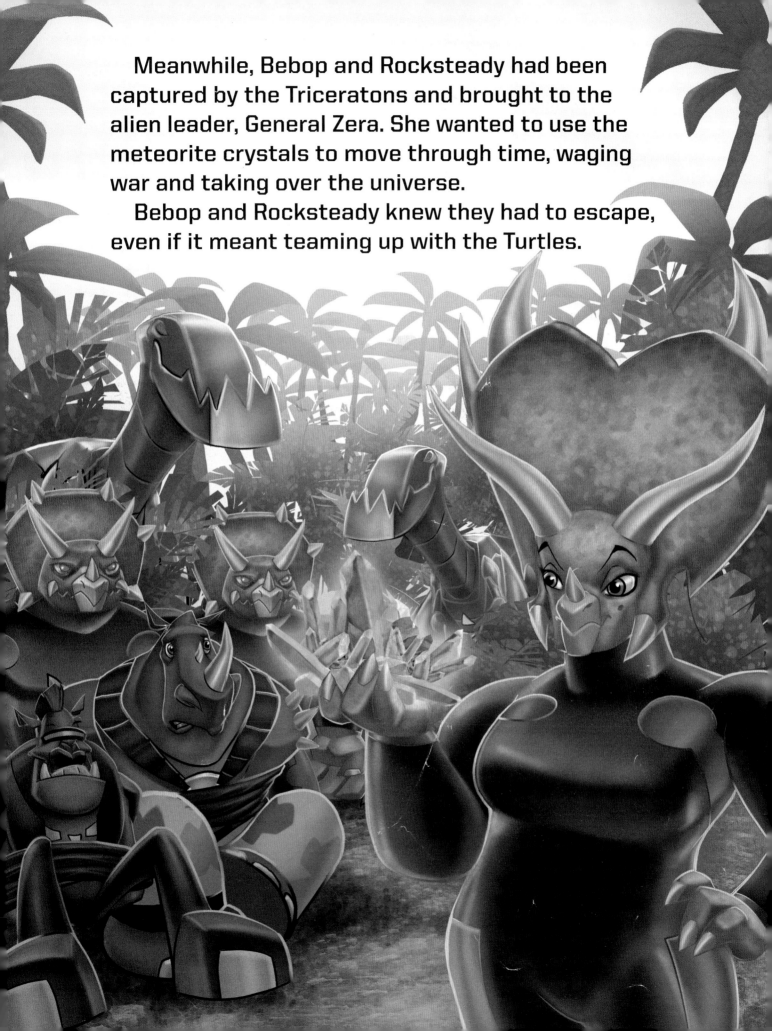

The Turtles knew that in order to get the crystals, they'd need some help from their dinosaur friends.

"Turtles and Dinos, to battle!" Leo shouted. *"Dino-bunga!"* Mikey yelled. He, Leo, and Donnie charged toward the Triceraton base on their dino-steeds.

As soon as the Turtles attacked the Triceraton base, the aliens unleashed their ultimate weapon—a giant Robo-Spinosaurus!

It was fierce and strong. The Turtles couldn't make a dent in it.

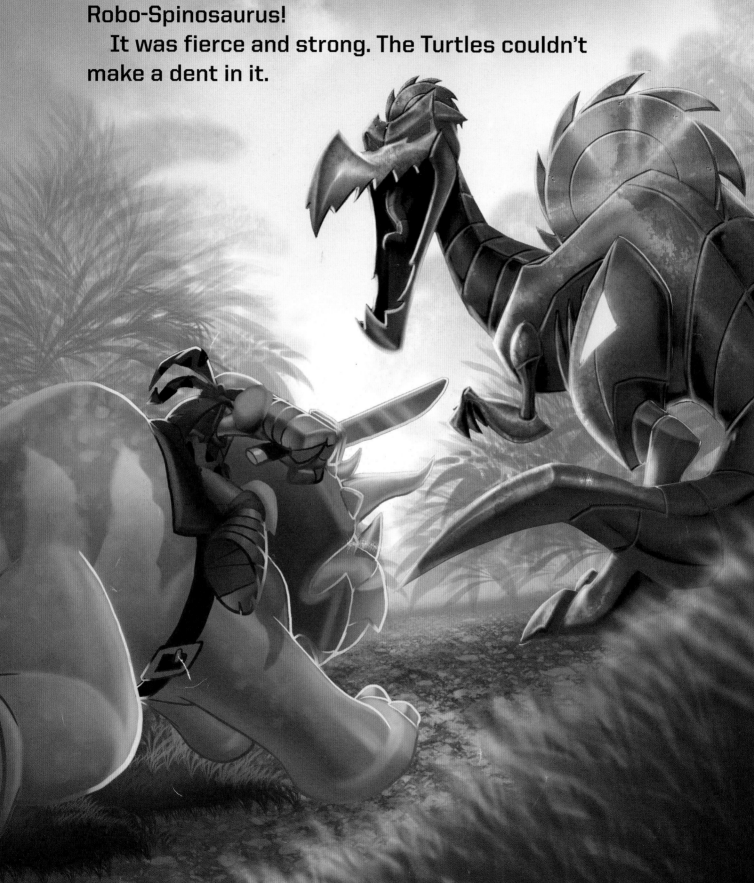

Suddenly, Raph swooped in on his pteranodon. It dropped a giant rock on the Robo-Spinosaurus.

The roaring robot crashed to the ground. The other Turtles rode in on their dino-steeds and finished it off.

As the Turtles galloped into the base, General Zera pointed her blaster at Donnie. Bebop sent it flying with a mighty kick.

Zera knew she was overwhelmed and commanded her troops to retreat.

Rocksteady asked for a ride back to the future. Leo nodded.

After the battle, Donnie inspected the damaged Shellformer. "I bet I can salvage parts from the Robo-Spinosaurus to fix the ship. The bigger problem will be calculating the—"

"Right," Leo said. "Just hurry."

Donnie went to work.

Three days later, the Turtles were ready to go. They said goodbye to their dinosaur friends and climbed aboard the repaired Shellformer with Bebop and Rocksteady.

"All right, team. Let's go home," Leo said, locking the ship's door.

Donnie switched to rocket-jet mode and they blasted off.

Whoosh! The Shellformer came to a stop. The Turtles stepped out and found themselves in New York City—in the distant future!

"That giant statue of Shredder can't be a good thing," Raph said.

Mikey pulled out his *nunchucks* and yelled, *"Booyakasha!"*

The Turtles were ready for their next adventure.